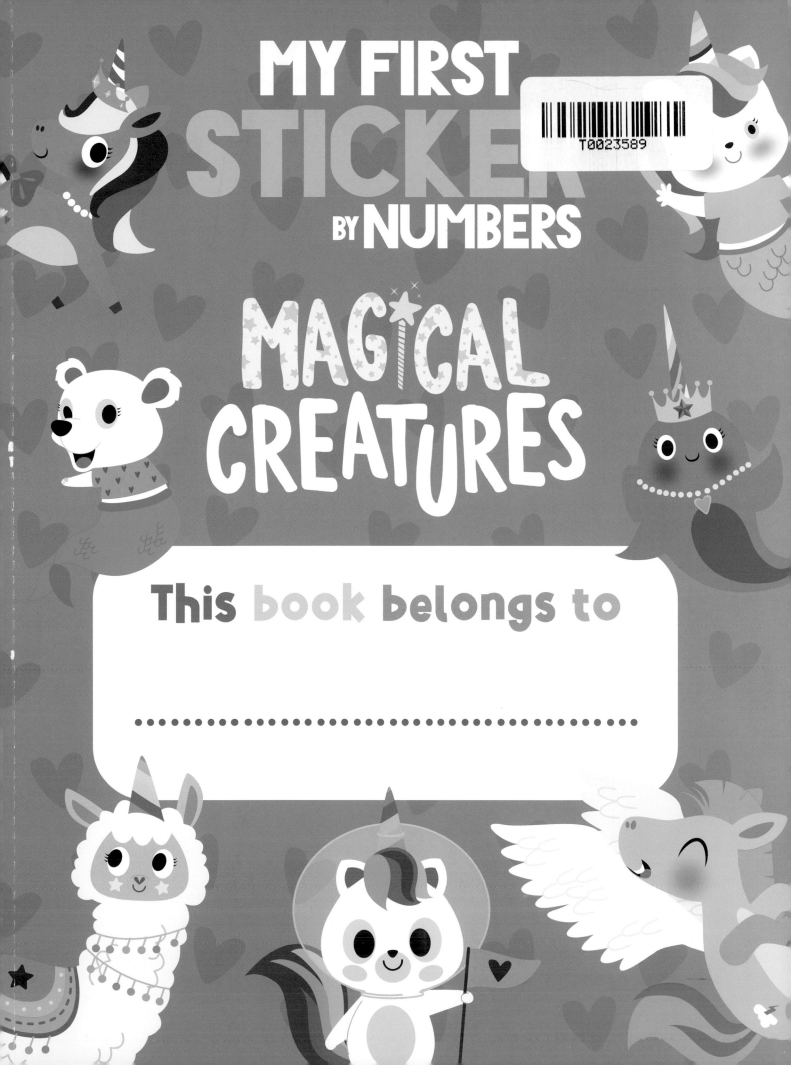

MY FIRST STICKER BY NUMBERS

MAGICAL CREATURES

This book belongs to

....

Are you ready to STICKER BY NUMBERS?

Step 1
Carefully tear out your picture.

Step 2
Find and tear out the matching sticker sheet at the back of the book.

Step 3
Match the numbers to create your picture.

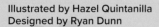

Step 4
Add your name and use the extra stickers to decorate your picture!

Illustrated by Hazel Quintanilla
Designed by Ryan Dunn

Copyright © Bidu Bidu Books Ltd 2022

Sourcebooks and the colophon are registered trademarks of Sourcebooks. All rights reserved.

Published by Sourcebooks Wonderland, an imprint of Sourcebooks Kids
P.O. Box 4410, Naperville, Illinois 60567-4410
(630) 961-3900
sourcebookskids.com

Date of Production: October 2023
Run Number: 5036540
Printed and bound in China (GD)
10 9 8 7 6 5 4 3

Picture by:

Picture by:

Picture by:

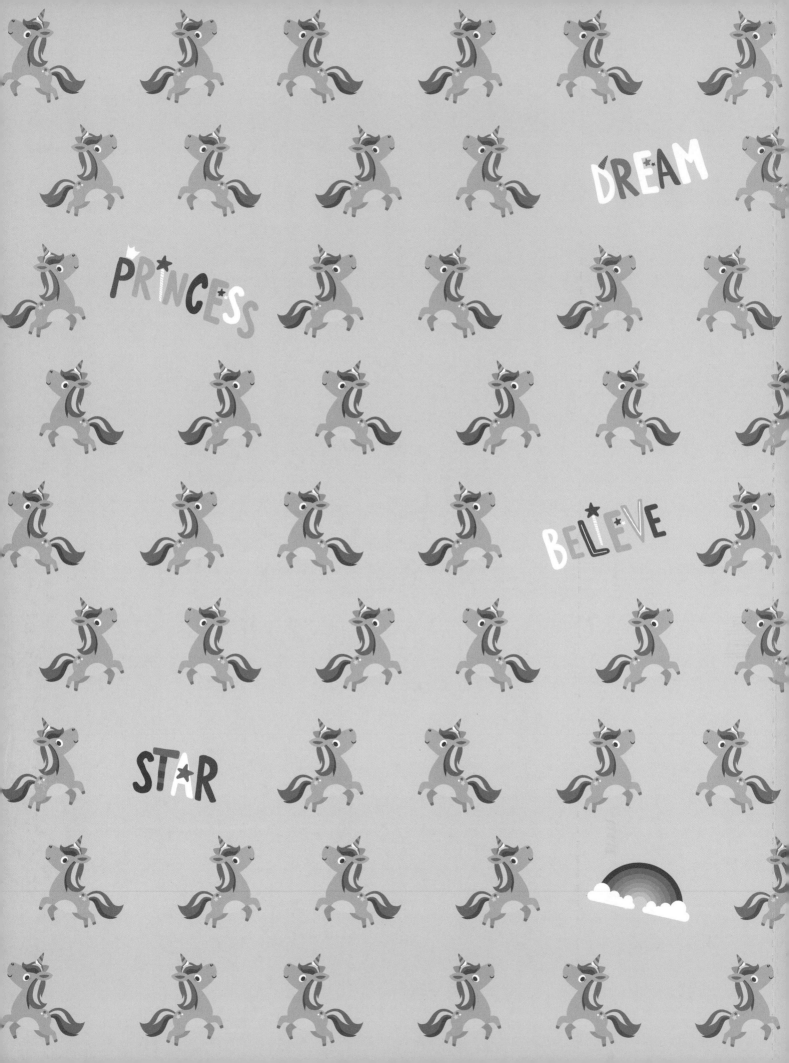

Picture by:

Picture by:

Picture by:

Picture by:

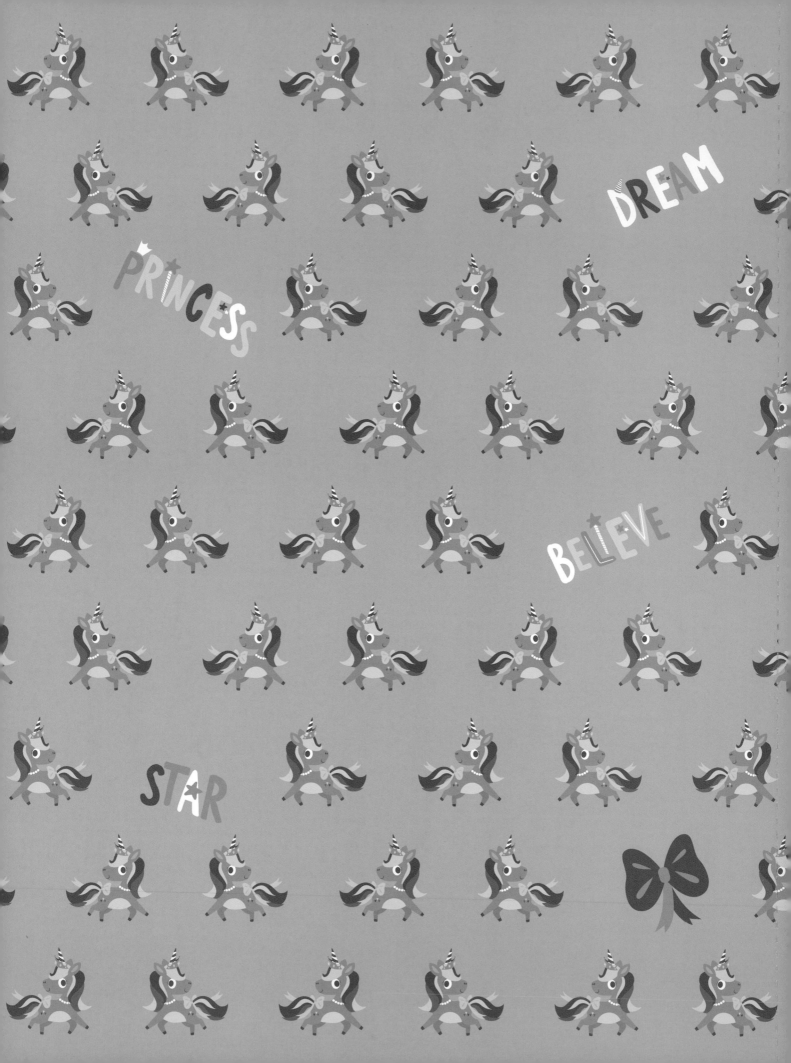

Picture by:

DREAM

PRINCESS

BELIEVE

STAR

Picture by:

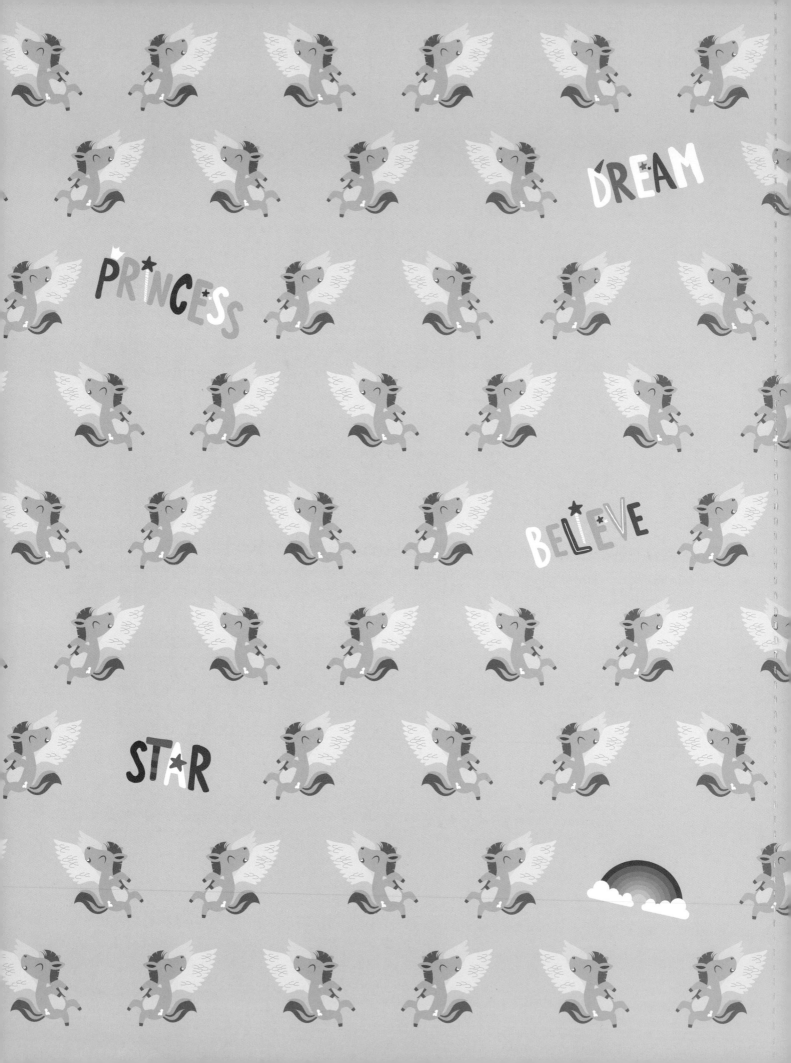

Picture by:

PRINCESS

TO GRANDMA